Forrest Gump

WINSTON GROOM

Level 3

Retold by John Escott
Series Editors: Andy Hopkins and Jocelyn Potter

D0869180

Pearson Education Limited
Edinburgh Gate, Harlow,
Essex CM20 2JE, England
and Associated Companies throughout the world.

ISBN: 978-1-4058-7675-9

First published in Great Britain by Black Swan 1994
This adaptation first published by Penguin Books Ltd 1996
Published by Addison Wesley Longman Ltd and Penguin Books Ltd 1998
New edition first published 1999
This edition first published 2008

11

Text copyright © John Escott 1996
Illustrations copyright © David Cuzik (Pennant Illustration Agency) 1996

The moral right of the adapter and of the illustrator has been asserted

Typeset by Graphicraft Ltd, Hong Kong
Set in 11/14pt Bembo
Printed in China
SWTC/11

Published by Pearson Education Ltd in association with
Penguin Books Ltd, both companies being subsidiaries of Pearson Plc

For a complete list of the titles available in the Penguin Readers series please write to your local
Pearson Longman office or to: Penguin Readers Marketing Department, Pearson Education,
Edinburgh Gate, Harlow, Essex CM20 2JE, England.

Contents

Introduction

One day when Curtis had to change a wheel on the car, I helped him.

'If you're an idiot,' he said angrily, 'how do you know how to do that?'

'Maybe I am an idiot,' I said, 'but I'm not stupid.'

'Gump' is an old English word for 'idiot'. In this warm, funny and sad story, we learn that an idiot may be cleverer than we think. Forrest Gump comes from Alabama, USA, and he sees the world through the eyes of a child. When people tell him things, he believes them. When they tell him to do things, he does them. But he gets through life with surprising success. He's a good football player, and he fights bravely in the Vietnam war. He is even sent into space with an ape called Sue. After the war, he starts a successful business. But will he get what he really wants – the girl he loves?

The film *Forrest Gump* came out in 1994. It was a big success in cinemas and won six Oscars. Tom Hanks won Best Actor, and the film won Best Picture. Sally Field also stars, as Forrest's mother. All through the film, Forrest sits at a bus stop, telling his life story to the person next to him. His story is also the story of America from the 1960s to the 1990s.

The writer, Winston Groom, grew up in Mobile, Alabama, which is Forrest Gump's home town. Like Forrest, Groom was a soldier in the army and fought in Vietnam. He wrote *Forrest Gump* in 1985. Some of his other books are *Better Times Than These* about the war in Vietnam, and *Gump and Co.*, a second story about Forrest Gump.

Chapter 1   School and Football

I was born an idiot – but I'm cleverer than people think. I can *think* things OK, but when I have to say them or write them down, sometimes they come out all wrong. When I was born, my Mom named me Forrest. My daddy died just after I was born. He worked on the ships. One day a big box of bananas fell down on my daddy and killed him.

I don't like bananas much. Only banana cake. I like that all right.

At first when I was growing up, I played with everybody. But then some boys hit me, and my Mom didn't want me to play with them again. I tried to play with girls, but they all ran away from me.

I went to an ordinary school for a year. Then the children started laughing and running away from me. But one girl, Jenny Curran, didn't run away, and sometimes she walked home with me. She was nice.

Then they put me into another kind of school, and there were some strange boys there. Some couldn't eat or go to the toilet without help. I stayed in that school for five or six years. But when I was thirteen, I grew six inches in six months! And by the time I was sixteen, I was bigger and heavier than all the other boys in the school.

One day I was walking home, and a car stopped next to me. The driver asked me my name, and I told him. 'What school do you go to?' he asked.

I told him about the idiot school.

'Do you ever play football?' he asked.

'No,' I told him. 'I see other people playing, but I don't play and they never ask me to play with them.'

'OK,' the man said.

Three days later, the man in the car came and got me out of

school. Mom was there, and they got all the things out of my desk and put them in a brown paper bag. Then they told me to say goodbye to the teacher.

The man in the car took me and Mom to the new high school. There, an old man with grey hair asked me lots of questions. But I knew that they *really* wanted me to play football. The man in the car was a football coach called Fellers. Coach Fellers asked me to put on a football suit, then asked me to undress and dress again, twenty times, until I could do it easily.

I began to play football with the high school team, and Coach Fellers helped me. And I went to lessons in the school. One teacher, Miss Henderson, was really nice. She taught me to read. And who do you think I saw in the school café? Jenny Curran! She was all grown-up now, with pretty black hair, long legs, and a beautiful face. I went and sat with her, and she remembered me!

But there was a boy in the café who started calling me names, and saying things like, 'How's Stupid?'. Then he threw some milk at me, and I jumped out of my chair and ran away. A day or two later, after school in the afternoon, he and his friends came up to me and started pushing and hitting me. Then they ran after me across the football field. I ran away fast!

I saw that Coach Fellers was watching me. He had a strange look on his face, and he came and told me to put on my football suit. That afternoon, he gave *me* the ball to run with. The others started running after me, and I ran as fast as I could. When they caught me, it needed eight of them to pull me down! Coach Fellers was really happy! He started jumping up and down and laughing. And after that, everybody liked me.

We had our first game, and I was frightened. But they gave me the ball, and I ran over the goal line two or three times. People were really kind to me after that!

Then something happened which was not so good.

'I want to take Jenny Curran to the cinema,' I told Mom one day.

*Then he threw some milk at me, and I jumped out
of my chair and ran away.*

So she phoned Jenny's Mom and explained. Next evening, Jenny arrived at our house, wearing a white dress, and with a pink flower in her hair. She was the prettiest thing that I ever saw.

The cinema was not far from our house. Jenny got the tickets, and we went inside. The film was about a man and a woman, Bonnie and Clyde, and there was a lot of shooting and killing. Well, I laughed a lot. But when I did this, people looked at me, and Jenny got down lower and lower in her place. Once I thought she was on the floor, and I put my hand on her shoulder to pull her up. But I pulled her dress, and it came open, and she screamed.

I tried to put my hands in front of her, because there were people looking at us. Then two men came and took me to an office. A few minutes later, four policemen arrived, and took me to the police station!

Mom came to the police station. She was crying, and I knew that I was in trouble again. And I *was* in trouble, but I was lucky. Next day, a letter arrived from a university. It was good news: if I played in their football team, there was a place for me in school there.

And the police said, 'That's OK with us. Just get out of town!'

So the next morning, Mom put some things into a suitcase for me, and put me on a bus. She was crying again. But they started the bus, and away I went.

Chapter 2   Life at University

When we got to the university, Coach Bryant came to talk to us.

'Last man to get to the practice field will get a ride there on my shoe!' he shouted at us. And he meant it when he said that kind of thing. We soon learned that.

The building that I went to live in was nice on the outside but not on the inside. Most of the doors and windows were broken, and the floor was dirty. I lived in a room with a man called Curtis. He

4

crashed into the room with a wild look in his eyes. He wasn't very tall, but he was very strong. 'Where are you from?' he asked.

'Mobile,' I told him.

'That's a stupid town!' he said.

And that was all of our conversation for several days.

On the practice field, things didn't start very well. I got the ball, but I ran the wrong way with it, and everybody got angry and started shouting at me.

But Coach Bryant called me across. 'Just get in the line and start catching the ball,' he told me.

And then I told him something that he didn't want to hear.

'They never taught me to catch a ball at high school,' I said. 'It was difficult enough for me just to remember where our goal line was.'

I don't think he was very pleased. But he started to teach me to catch.

I wanted my Mom, and I wanted to go home. I didn't like that place.

And Curtis was always angry, and I couldn't understand him. He had a car, and sometimes he gave me a ride to the practice field. But one day when he had to change a wheel on the car, I helped him.

'If you're an idiot,' he said, angrily, 'how do you know how to do that?'

'Maybe I am an idiot,' I said, 'but I'm not *stupid*.'

Then Curtis ran after me, and called me all kinds of terrible names.

After that, I moved my bed to another room.

♦

The first football game was on Saturday. I ran well, and we won 35 to 3. Everybody was pleased with me. I phoned Mom to tell her.

'I heard the game on the radio!' she said. 'I was so happy, I wanted to cry!'

5

That night, everybody went to parties, but nobody asked me to go. I went back to my room, but I heard music from somewhere upstairs. I found a young man who was sitting in his room playing the harmonica.

His name was Bubba. He broke his foot in football practice and couldn't play in the game. I sat and listened to him. We didn't talk, but after about an hour, I asked, 'Can I try it?' and he said 'OK', and gave me the harmonica. I began to play.

After several minutes, Bubba was getting really excited and saying, 'Good, good, good!' Then he asked, 'Where did you learn to play like that?'

'I didn't learn anywhere,' I said.

When it got late, he told me to take the harmonica with me, and I played it for a long time in my room.

*I found a young man who was sitting in his room
playing the harmonica.*

Next day I took it back to Bubba.

'Keep it,' he said. 'I've got another one.'

I was really happy, and I went and sat under a tree and played all day.

It was late afternoon when I began to walk back to my room. Suddenly, I heard a voice shout, 'Forrest!' I turned round – and saw Jenny!

She had a big smile on her face, and she held my hand.

'I saw you play football yesterday,' she said. 'You were wonderful!'

She wasn't angry about the cinema, and she asked me to have a drink with her!

'I'm taking lessons in music, and I want to be a singer,' she told me. 'I play in a little group. We're playing at the Students' Centre tomorrow night. Why don't you come and listen?'

'OK,' I said.

Chapter 3   The Big Game

On Friday night, I went to the Students' Centre. There were a lot of people there, and Jenny was wearing a long dress and singing. Three or four other people were in the group with her, and they made a good sound. Jenny saw me and smiled, and I sat on the floor and listened. It was wonderful.

They played for about an hour, and I was lying back with my eyes closed, listening happily. How did it happen? I'm not sure. But suddenly I found that I was playing my harmonica with them!

Jenny stopped singing for a second or two, and the others in the group stopped playing. Then Jenny laughed and began to sing with my harmonica, and then everybody was saying 'Wonderful!' to me.

Jenny came to see me. 'Forrest, where did you learn to play that thing?'

'I didn't learn anywhere,' I told her.

Well, after that, Jenny asked me to play with their group every Friday, and paid me $25 every time!

♦

The only other important thing that happened to me at the university was the Big Game at the Orange Bowl in Miami that year. It was an important game which Coach Bryant wanted us to win.

The game started, and the ball came to me. I took it – and ran straight into a group of big men on the other team! Crash! It was like that all afternoon.

When they were winning 28 to 7, Coach Bryant called me across. 'Forrest,' he said, 'all year we have secretly taught you to catch the ball and run with it. Now you're going to run like a wild animal. OK?'

'OK, Coach,' I said.

And I did. Everybody was surprised to see that I could catch the ball. Suddenly it was 28 to 14! And after I caught it four or five more times, it was 28 to 21. Then the other team got two men to run after me. But that meant Gwinn was free to catch the ball, and he put us on the 15-yard line. Then Weasel, the kicker, got a field goal, and it was 28 to 24!

But then things began to go wrong again. Weasel made a bad mistake – and then the game finished, and we were the losers.

Coach Bryant wasn't very happy. 'Well, boys,' he said, 'there's always next year.'

But not for me. I soon learned that.

♦

I couldn't stay at the university. I wasn't clever enough at the lessons, and there was nothing that anybody could do about it. Coach Bryant was very sad.

'I knew this would happen, Forrest,' he said. 'But I said to them,

I took it — and ran straight into a group of big men on the other team!

"Just give me that boy in my team for a year!", and they did. And we had a good year – the best year, Forrest! Good luck, boy!'

Bubba helped me to put my things in my suitcase, then he walked to the bus with me to say goodbye. We went past the Students' Centre. But it wasn't Friday night, and Jenny's band wasn't playing. I didn't know where she was.

It was late when the bus got to Mobile. Mom knew that I was coming, but she was crying when I got home.

'What's wrong?' I asked.

'A letter came,' she cried. 'You've got to go in the army!'

Chapter 4   Vietnam

After I left the idiot school, people were always shouting at me – Coach Fellers, Coach Bryant, and then the people in the army. But I have to say this: the people in the army shouted louder and longer than anybody!

Fort Benning was in Georgia. After about a hundred hours on a bus, me and a lot of other new young soldiers arrived there. The place where I had to live was just a bit better than the rooms at the university, but the food was not. It was terrible.

Then, and in the months to come, I just had to do the things that I was told to do. They taught me how to shoot guns, throw hand grenades, and move along the ground on my stomach.

One day, the cook was ill, and somebody said, 'Gump, you're going to be the cook today.'

'What am I going to cook?' I said. '*How* do I cook?'

'It's easy,' said one of the men. 'Just put everything that you see in the food cupboard into a big pot and cook it.'

'Maybe it won't taste very good,' I said.

'Nothing *does* in this place!' he said. He was right.

Well, I got tins of tomatoes, some rice, apples, potatoes, and everything that I could find. 'What am I going to cook it in?' I asked one of the men.

'There are some pots in the cupboard,' he said. But the pots were only small.

'You've got to find something,' one of the other men said.

'What about this?' I asked. There was a big metal thing about six feet tall and five feet round, sitting in the corner.

'That's the boiler. You can't cook anything in that.'

'Why not?' I asked. 'It's hot. It's got water in it.'

But the men had other things to do. 'Do what you like,' they said.

So I used the boiler.

I put everything in it, and after about an hour you could smell the cooking. It smelled OK. Then the men came back and everybody was waiting for their dinner.

'Hurry up with that food, Gump! We're hungry!' they shouted.

Suddenly, the boiler began to shake and make noises – and then it blew up!

It blew the food all over us – me, and all the men who were sitting at the tables.

'Gump!' they screamed. 'You're an idiot!'

But I already knew that.

◆

After a year, we went to Vietnam to fight in the war. One evening we went to have a shower. The 'showers' were just a long hole in the ground for us to stand in, while somebody threw water over us. We were standing in it, when suddenly there was a strange noise.

Then the ground began to blow up all round us!

We threw ourselves on to the floor of the shower hole, and somebody started screaming. It was some of our men on the far side of the hole, and there was blood all over them. Then everything

11

went quiet again, and after a minute or two the rest of us climbed up out of the hole.

The enemy soldiers tried to blow us up for the next five nights, then it stopped. But it was time for us to move up north to help some of our other men in the jungle.

We went in helicopters, and there was smoke coming up out of the jungle when we got there. The enemy started shooting at us before we got on the ground, and they blew up one of our helicopters. It was terrible! People on fire, and nothing that we could do. It was almost night before we found our other soldiers in the jungle.

And who do you think one of them was? It was Bubba!

Well, in between the shooting, Bubba told me about himself. His foot got too bad to play football, and he had to leave the university. But his foot wasn't too bad for the army to get him – and here he was.

'What happened to Jenny Curran?' I asked.

'She left school and went off with a group of people who were against the war,' he said.

Chapter 5   Danger in the Jungle

There was a little valley between two hills. We were on one hill and the enemy was on the other. Then we got orders to move the machine gun about fifty metres to the left of the big tree that was in the middle of the valley, and to find a safe place to put it before the enemy blew us all up.

We found a place to put the gun and stayed there all night. We could hear shooting all round us, but they didn't hit us. When it was day again, our planes came, and they blew up the enemy soldiers. Then we watched while our men moved off the hill and came down into the valley.

The enemy started shooting at us before we got on the ground, and they blew up one of our helicopters.

Suddenly, somebody started shooting at them! We couldn't see the enemy soldiers because the jungle was too thick, but *somebody* was shooting at our men.

The shooting was *in front* of us, which meant that the enemy soldiers were in between us and our men. And this meant that the enemy was able to come back and find us, so we had to get out fast.

We began to move back to the hill, but Doyle suddenly saw more enemy soldiers who were going towards our men! We waited until they got to the top, then Bones began shooting with the machine gun. He probably killed ten or fifteen enemy soldiers. Doyle and I and the other two men threw grenades, but then an enemy soldier shot Bones in the head. I pulled the machine gun from his hands, and shouted to Doyle.

There was no answer.

Two of them were dead, and Doyle was only just alive.

I picked up Doyle and put him across my shoulders, then I ran towards the hill. There were bullets flying all round me from behind – and then I saw more enemy soldiers in the low grass in front of me! They were shooting at our men on the hill.

I ran fast, shouting and screaming as loudly as I could. And suddenly I was in the middle of our soldiers, and everybody was pleased and hitting me on the back! My shouting and screaming frightened the enemy soldiers away. They just ran!

♦

The weeks went past slowly. I got a letter from my Mom, and I wrote back to her that everything was OK. I also wrote a letter to Jenny Curran and asked Mom to ask her parents to send it on to her. But I didn't get a reply.

Bubba and I decided that we would get a shrimp boat when we got home again, and catch shrimps, and make a lot of money. Bubba planned it all.

It started to rain one day, and it didn't stop for two months! But

I ran fast, shouting and screaming as loudly as I could.

we still had to look for enemy soldiers – and one day we found them. We were crossing a rice field when suddenly they started shooting at us. Somebody shouted, 'Back!' I picked up my machine gun and ran towards some trees.

I looked round for Bubba, but he wasn't there. Then I heard that he was out in the rice field, and he was hurt, so I left my gun by the trees and ran back into the field. 'Gump! You can't go out there!' somebody shouted. But I just ran.

Halfway out, I saw another man who was hurt. He was holding a hand up to me – so I picked him up and ran back to the trees with him. Then I ran out again and found Bubba. There was blood all over him and he had two bullets in his stomach.

He looked up at me, and said, 'Forrest, why did this happen?' What could I say? Then he said, 'Play me a song on the harmonica, will you?'

There was still a lot of shooting going on, but I played a song. Then all the colour went out of Bubba's face and he said something very softly: '*Home*.'

And then he died.

And that's all I've got to say about that.

♦

The rest of the night was terrible. The worst night that I've ever known. Nobody could get any help to us, and the enemy soldiers were so near that we could hear them talking. Then, when it got light, an American plane came and used fire-throwers on the enemy – and almost on us! Suddenly the trees were on fire, and men were running out of the jungle with burned skin and clothes.

During all of this, somebody shot me in the back of the leg, but I can't remember when it happened. It didn't matter. Nothing mattered. Bubba was dead, the shrimp business idea was dead with him. I just wanted to die, too.

Then our helicopters came, and the enemy soldiers who were left ran away.

An hour later, I was out of there and on my way to the hospital in Danang.

Chapter 6   The White House

I was at the hospital for two months. After the first few weeks my leg was getting better, and one day I went down into the little town, to the fish market. I bought some shrimps, and one of the cooks at the hospital cooked them for me. Two days later, I went back to the fish market and talked to a man who was selling shrimps.

'Where do you get them?' I asked him.

He immediately started talking fast in a language that I couldn't understand, but he took me somewhere – past all the boats and the beach. There he took a net and put it in the water. When he took it out again, it was full of shrimps!

Every day for the next few weeks, I went with Mr Chi (that was his name) and watched him while he worked. He showed me how to catch shrimps with the net, and it was so easy that an idiot was able to do it!

Which I did!

Then one day I got back to the hospital and a Colonel Gooch said, 'Gump, we're going back to America together! You're going to see the President of the United States, and he's going to give you a medal because you were very brave.'

♦

There were about two thousand people waiting for us at San Francisco airport when we got off the plane! What a surprise! A lot of them had beards and long hair. I thought perhaps they were there to welcome us, but I was wrong. They were shouting unpleasant

17

*He showed me how to catch shrimps with the net, and it was so easy
that an idiot was able to do it!*

things, and then somebody threw a tomato at Colonel Gooch and it hit him in the face. He tried to clean it off and not look angry, but I didn't want to wait for them to start throwing things at me! No sir! I started running.

The people ran after me – all two thousand of them! – but they couldn't catch me. I ran all round the airport, and then I ran into a toilet and locked the door. I waited in there for almost an hour before I came out again.

I went to look for Colonel Gooch, and I found him in the middle of a group of policemen. He was looking very worried until he saw me.

'Come on, Gump!' he said. 'The plane for Washington is waiting for us.'

The army sent a car to meet us at Washington airport, and we drove to a really nice hotel. After we put our suitcases in our rooms, the Colonel asked me to go out to a bar with him for a drink.

'People are different here,' he told me. 'They aren't like the people in California.'

He was wrong.

When we got there, he bought me a beer, and he was telling me about the President and my medal when something happened. A pretty girl came up to our table, and the Colonel thought she was a waitress.

'Get us two more drinks, please,' he said.

She looked at him and said, 'I won't get you anything – not as much as a glass of warm river-water, you pig!' Then she looked at me and said, 'And how many babies have you killed today, you big ape?'

Well, after that we went back to the hotel.

♦

Next morning we got up early and went to the White House, where the President lives. It's a really pretty house with a big garden.

A lot of army people were there, and they immediately started shaking my hand and telling me that I was a brave man and that they were pleased to meet me.

The President was a great big old man who talked like somebody from Texas, and there were a lot of people standing round him in the flower garden.

Then an army man started to read something, and everybody listened. Everybody but me, because I was hungry and wanted some breakfast. At last the army man finished reading, and then the President came up and gave me the medal. After that, he began to shake my hand.

I was just thinking of getting out of there and having some breakfast when the President said, 'Boy, is that your stomach making that noise?' So I said, 'Yes,' and the President said, 'Well, come on, boy, let's go and get something to eat!' And I followed him into the house, and a waiter got us some breakfast.

The President asked me a lot of questions about Vietnam and the army, but I just said, 'Yes, it's OK' or shook my head to say no, and after several minutes of this we were both silent.

'Do you want to watch TV?' the President asked suddenly.

So me and the President of America watched TV while I ate my breakfast!

Later, when we were back in the garden, the President said, 'You were hurt, weren't you, boy? Well, look at this . . .' And he pulled up his shirt and showed me the place on his stomach where he was hurt once. 'Where were you hurt?' he asked me.

So I pulled down my trousers, turned round and showed him.

Well, lots of newspaper men started taking photographs before Colonel Gooch could run across and pull me away!

That afternoon, back at the hotel, he came to my room shouting and throwing newspapers on to the bed. And there I was, on the front page, with my trousers down!

'Gump, you idiot!' shouted Colonel Gooch.

. . . and then the President came up and gave me the medal.

'Yes, sir,' I said. 'That's what I am. But I just try to do the right thing.'

Chapter 7   Meeting Jenny Again

Soon after that, I heard that I was leaving the army early, and they gave me some money for a train ticket to go home.

But all this time, I was thinking about Jenny Curran. Just before I left the hospital in Danang, I had a letter from her. She was now playing in a group called The Broken Eggs, and they played two nights each week at a place called the Hodaddy Club near Harvard University. Now that I was free from the army, I just wanted to go and see her. So I got a ticket for Boston, instead of Mobile.

I tried to walk to the Hodaddy Club from the train station, but I lost my way, so I took a taxi. It was in the afternoon, and the man behind the bar said, 'Jenny'll be here about nine o'clock.'

'Can I wait?' I asked.

'OK,' he said.

So I sat down and waited for five or six hours.

Students began to come in, most of them wearing dirty jeans. The men had beards, and the women had long, untidy hair. Later, the group – The Broken Eggs – arrived, but I didn't see Jenny. Then they began to play – and they were *loud*. The music sounded like a plane that was taking off! But the students loved it.

And then Jenny came on!

She was different. Her hair was all the way down her back, and she was wearing sun-glasses – at night! She was wearing blue jeans and a shirt with lots of colours on it. The group started playing again and Jenny began to sing.

Later, I went outside and walked round for about half an hour, then went back. There were a lot of people waiting to go in, so I went round to the back of the place and sat on the ground. I had my harmonica in my pocket, so I took it out and started to play.

I had my harmonica in my pocket, so I took it out and started to play.

I could hear the music that was playing inside and, after a minute or two, I began playing with it. Suddenly, a door behind me opened – and there was Jenny!

'Who is that playing the harmonica?' she said. And then she saw me. '*Forrest Gump!*' And she ran out of the door and threw her arms round me.

♦

We talked together until it was time for her to sing again.

'I didn't leave school,' said Jenny. 'They threw me out after they found a boy in my room one night. I went to California and stayed there for some time.' She laughed. 'I wore flowers in my hair, and talked about love. But the people that I was with were strange. Then I met a man, and we came to Boston. But he was dangerous. He was against the war, like me, but he blew up buildings and things. I couldn't stay with him. Next, I met a teacher from Harvard University, but he was married. Then I began to sing with The Broken Eggs.'

'Where do you live?' I asked.

'With my boyfriend,' she said. 'He's a student. You can come back and stay with us tonight.'

The boyfriend's name was Rudolph. He was a little man, and he was sitting on the floor with his eyes shut when we got to Jenny's flat.

'Rudolph, this is Forrest,' Jenny said. 'He's a friend of mine from home, and he's going to stay with us for a few days.'

Rudolph didn't speak or open his eyes, but he put up his hand and smiled.

Next morning, when I got up, Rudolph was still sitting on the floor with his eyes shut.

That afternoon, Jenny took me to meet the other people in the group, and that night I began playing my harmonica with them at the Hodaddy Club. It went well, and I played with them every night after that.

Then one day I came back to the flat and Jenny was sitting on the floor.

'Where's Rudolph?' I asked.

'Gone,' she said. 'Walked out, like all the others.' And then she started to cry.

'Don't cry, Jenny,' I said. And I put my arm round her.

Well, it started like that. But the next minute we were kissing and making love! And when we finished, Jenny said, 'Forrest, where have you *been* all this time?'

Chapter 8   Into Space

Spring and summer went by, and I continued to play my harmonica with the group. It was my happiest time of all. But – you've guessed it – something went wrong.

How did it happen? I don't know. But one night I was sitting outside the Hodaddy Club, smoking a cigarette, when a girl smiled and came up to me. She sat down across my legs and put her arms round me. She was laughing and kissing me, and I didn't know what to do.

Suddenly, the door opened behind me, and there was Jenny.

'Forrest, it's time to –' She stopped when she saw me with the girl. Then she said, 'Oh, no! Not you, too!'

I jumped up and pushed the girl away. 'Jenny!' I said.

'Stay away from me, Forrest!' she said. 'You men are all the same! Just stay away from me!'

She didn't speak to me again that night. And the next morning she told me to find another place to live.

I went to live with Moses, one of the other men in the group, and soon after that Jenny went to Washington to talk and work against the war. Moses wrote down the address for me.

So I went back to Washington, too.

Suddenly Jenny said, 'Did you know that Forrest won a medal?'

There was a lot of trouble there. Police were everywhere, and people were shouting and throwing things.

And the police were taking some of them away.

I went to find Jenny's address, but there was nobody at home. I waited outside for most of the day. Then, at about nine o'clock, a car stopped near the house and some people got out. And there she was!

I started to walk towards her, but she turned and walked away. The other people – two men and a girl – didn't know what to say.

'What's wrong with her?' I asked one of the two men.

'She just got out of prison,' he said. 'She was there all night before we could get her out.'

Jenny was in the back of the car now, so I went over and talked to her through the window. I told her how I felt – I was sorry about the girl, and I didn't want to play in the group without her. She listened quietly, then opened the car door for me to get in, and we sat and talked.

The others were talking about something that would happen the next day. Some American soldiers planned to take off their Vietnam medals and throw them away in front of the crowds of people.

Suddenly Jenny said, 'Did you know that Forrest won a medal?'

The others went quiet and looked at me, then looked at Jenny.

♦

Next morning, Jenny came into the living-room. I was sleeping on the floor of their house. She woke me up.

'Forrest,' she said. 'I want you to do something for me.'

'What?' I said.

'I want you to come with us today, and I want you to wear your army clothes.'

'Why?' I asked.

'Because you're going to do something to stop all the killing in Vietnam.'

27

You can guess what I had to do, can't you? I had to throw away my medal with the other American soldiers. But because my medal was a more famous medal than theirs, it was more important to Jenny and her friends.

But it got me into more trouble. Oh, I threw my medal away, OK – but it hit somebody really important! One of the President's men! So they threw me into prison.

Why do things like that always happen to me?

♦

As it happened, I didn't stay in prison long, because they soon realized that I was an idiot, and they put me in a special hospital for idiots.

It was the doctors at the hospital who decided to send me to NASA – that's the space centre at Houston, in Texas.

'You're just the kind of person that they're looking for!' the doctors told me.

I soon understood why! NASA sent me on a journey into space with a woman and an ape! Me, a spaceman! It was very strange.

All kinds of things went wrong because of that ape. Instead of coming down in the sea when we returned, the space ship came down in the jungle somewhere, and it was four years before the NASA people found us! But the ape and I were soon good friends. His name was Sue (yes, I know it's a girl's name, but they sent a male ape up by mistake, and NASA didn't like to tell the newspapers that). And it was in the jungle that I met Big Sam – a man who taught me to play chess. And that was important, as you will see later.

Chapter 9   A Real Idiot

Of course, the first thing that I wanted to do when I got back to America was find Jenny. So I phoned Moses in Boston.

'The Broken Eggs group has broken up,' he told me. 'I don't know what happened to Jenny. I heard that she went to Chicago, but that was five years ago.'

'Do you have a telephone number, or anything?' I asked.

'It's an old number,' he said, 'but perhaps she's still there.'

I phoned the number, and she wasn't.

'Jenny Curran?' a man's voice said. 'She went to Indianapolis. Got a job at the Temperer factory.'

So I went to Indianapolis on the bus.

♦

The Temperer factory was outside the town. I asked about Jenny at the office, and the woman said, 'Yes, she works in here. Why don't you wait at the side of the factory? It's almost lunch-time, and she'll probably come out.' So I did.

A lot of people came out at lunch-time. Then Jenny came out. She went and sat under a tree on the grass, and began eating an apple. I went up behind her and said, 'That looks like a nice apple.' She didn't look up. She just said, 'Forrest, it has to be you.'

A minute later, I had my arms round her and we were both crying. People were watching us with strange looks on their faces, but it didn't matter. Jenny and me were together again.

'I finish work in three hours, Forrest,' Jenny said. 'Why don't you wait for me in that bar across the street? Then I'll take you to my place.'

So I waited in the bar.

And I got into the wrestling business. How? I'll tell you.

It started when I arm-wrestled a man in the bar, and won some money on a bet. That gave me an idea. But at first I didn't say anything to Jenny.

She came across to the bar after work, and we had a drink and talked.

'I saw you on TV when you went up into space, Forrest,' she said.

29

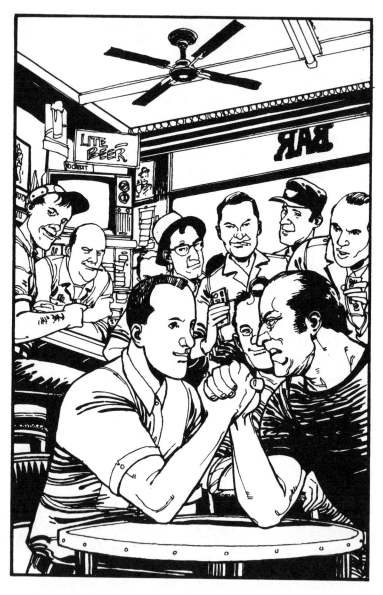

It started when I arm-wrestled a man in the bar, and won some money on a bet.

And I told her all about that, and about Sue, the ape.

'What happened to him?' she asked.

'I don't know,' I said. 'But he was a good friend.'

Later, we went back to Jenny's flat, and she said, 'You can stay here.'

Next day, when Jenny went to work, I went back to the bar. Several people wanted to try arm-wrestling with me again, and I said OK. None of them won because I was too strong, but plenty of people wanted to try their luck.

After about a month, I was winning nearly two hundred dollars a week, arm-wrestling. Then one day a man called Mike came into the bar.

'You can make a lot more money,' he told me.

'How?' I asked.

'Wrestling. *Real* wrestling,' he said. 'I can teach you.'

To make a long story short – he did.

Jenny wasn't happy about the wrestling but I won a lot of money – sometimes by winning fights, sometimes by losing them because Mike told me to lose them. Yes, that happens, too. But then I did something stupid again. I bet on myself *winning* a fight, after Mike told me to *lose* it.

Jenny got really angry. 'It isn't honest,' she said.

I didn't listen. I bet all my money on myself to win – and then I lost the fight.

But there was worse to come. When I got back to the flat, Jenny was gone, and there was a letter waiting for me. It said:

Dear Forrest

You're doing something bad tonight. It isn't honest, and I cannot go on with you like this. I think about having a house and a family and things like that now. I watched you grow up big and strong and good. And then, in Boston, I realized that I loved you, and I was the happiest girl in the world. But then there was that girl outside the Hodaddy Club. Then you went up into space and I lost you for four years, and I think you changed. And I think perhaps I changed, too. I just want to live in an ordinary way now. So, I must go and find it.

I am crying while I write this, but please don't try to find me. Goodbye, my dear.

love,

Jenny

And for the first time ever, I knew that I was a *real* idiot.

Chapter 10   Money for Playing Games

I decided to go home to Mobile, but the bus stopped at Nashville on the way and I went into town for a drink and something to eat. I was going past a hotel when I looked in the window and saw some people who were playing chess. Like I said before, Big Sam taught me how to play chess when I was in the jungle. Well, I went into the hotel to watch them, but it was a special chess tournament and it cost five dollars to watch, so I didn't go into the chess room.

I was just walking out again when I saw a little old man who was playing chess with himself at a table near the door. I had another hour before I had to catch the bus again, so I went across and watched him. Then I said, 'If you make that move, you'll lose your queen.'

He didn't look up but, after a minute, he said, 'Perhaps you're right.'

It was time for me to get back to the bus station, but when I started to leave, the old man said, 'Why don't you sit down and finish this game with me?'

'I can't,' I said. 'I have to catch a bus.'

So he waved at me with his hand, and I went back to the bus station.

It took me an hour to win that chess game.

But I missed the bus that evening, and there wasn't another one until the next day. So I walked back to the hotel, and there was the little old man, still playing against himself. He looked up and saw me, and told me to sit down.

It took me an hour to win that chess game.

'Just who *are* you?' he said after the game.

'Forrest Gump,' I said.

'Where did you learn to play chess?' he asked.

'In the jungle,' I told him.

He looked surprised. 'Aren't you in the tournament?' he asked.

'No,' I told him. 'I'm going home, and I'm going to start a shrimp business.'

'You can make a lot of money from chess,' he said. 'You're very good.'

'Am I?' I said.

The old man's name was Mr Tribble. Two days later we were on our way to Los Angeles, to a big chess tournament.

♦

We were a day or two early for the tournament, and Mr Tribble took me to see some people who were making a film. They make a lot of films in Los Angeles. We were watching a man who was crashing through a window in a film fight, when a man walked over to us.

'Are you an actor?' he asked me.

'Who, me?' I said.

'We're here for the chess tournament,' said Mr Tribble.

But the other man was looking at me. 'You *are* a big, strong man, aren't you?' he said. 'You're just what I need for a film that I'm making. My name is Felder.'

'He has to play chess in a tournament tomorrow,' said Mr Tribble. 'He hasn't got time to be an actor.'

'It won't take long,' said Mr Felder.

So we went with Mr Felder, and I found myself acting in a film about the jungle – with Raquel Welch, the famous film star!

'Is that *really* Raquel Welch?' I asked Mr Felder.

But things did not go well. Somehow, when I was helping Miss Welch to escape from the jungle, her dress came off and I had to run into the trees to hide her. But who do you think we met there? Sue, the ape! He was in *another* film!

The three of us ran out of there fast, and Miss Welch shouted and screamed.

No, things didn't go very well. I wasn't an actor for very long.

I think Mr Tribble was secretly pleased.

I was pleased because I was back with Sue again.

♦

Back at our hotel, the three of us sat in our room and tried to decide what to do.

'It's going to be difficult travelling with an ape,' said Mr Tribble.

34

'He won't be any trouble, Mr Tribble,' I said.

But Mr Tribble seemed worried.

Next day was the big chess tournament at the Beverly Hills Hotel. Mr Tribble and I got there early, and I had to play chess all day.

It took me about seven minutes to win the first game, and half an hour to win the next. I played all that day, and the next. And suddenly I was in the final, playing with a Russian, Honest Ivan, the best player in the world. He was a big man, with long black hair, and he didn't want to lose!

It was a long game. Honest Ivan was good – very good. But just when Honest Ivan seemed to be winning, *Sue ran across the room and jumped onto the chess table!*

Honest Ivan fell off his chair, and everybody started screaming and running everywhere. 'Let's get out of here, Forrest!' shouted Mr Tribble.

We got back to the hotel and hurried up to our room.

'Forrest,' said Mr Tribble, 'You're a wonderful chess player, but I never know what's going to happen next! Here's half of the money that you've won – it's almost five thousand dollars. Take Sue back to Alabama with you, and start your shrimp business.' He shook my hand and gave me his address. 'Write to me sometimes, Forrest. Good luck!'

Chapter 11   The Shrimp Business

Well, I finally went home to Mobile again. The train got into Mobile station about three o'clock in the morning, and Sue and I got off. We walked into the town and finally found a place to sleep in an empty building.

The next morning I bought some breakfast and got Sue some bananas to eat. Then we went to see Mom. She was pleased to see me.

Sue ran across the room and jumped onto the chess table!

'Oh, Forrest,' she said, 'you're home at last!'

'Yes, Mom,' I said.

But I didn't stay long. Two days later, Sue and I got the bus to Bayou La Batre, where Bubba's parents lived, and I explained to Bubba's daddy about the shrimp business that Bubba and I planned to start after we came out of the army. He listened, and he was very interested. And the next day he took Sue and me out in his little boat, to look for a good place to start the shrimp business.

It took almost a month to start things up – to get nets, and a boat, and everything. Finally the day came when Sue and I were ready to go shrimping. And by that night we had hundreds and hundreds of shrimps in our nets!

It was the beginning of my shrimp business. We worked hard, all that summer, and that autumn and winter and the next spring. And after a year, Mom was working for me, and Mr Tribble, and Curtis (my old football friend), and Bubba's daddy.

At the end of that year, we had thirty thousand dollars!

Everybody was very happy. But me? I was thinking of Jenny, of course. I wanted to find her again. And one day I dressed in my best clothes and got the bus to Mobile, and I went to Jenny's Mom's house.

'Forrest Gump!' she said, when she saw me. 'Come on in!'

Well, we talked about Mom and the shrimp business and everything. Then I asked about Jenny.

'I don't hear from her very often,' she said. 'I think they live somewhere in North Carolina now.'

'They?' I said.

'Didn't you know?' she said. 'Jenny married two years ago.'

♦

Why wasn't I ready for that news? I don't know, but I wasn't. And part of me seemed to die when I heard it. But Jenny only did what she had to do. Because I'm an idiot. A lot of people *say* that they married an idiot, but they don't know what it's like to marry a real one. I cried that night, but it didn't help.

'I'm just going to work hard,' I told myself. 'It's all I can do.'

And I did. And at the end of that year we had seventy-five thousand dollars.

♦

Time went on. I looked in the mirror and saw lines on my face and grey in my hair. The business was doing well, but I asked myself, 'What are you doing all this *for*?' And I knew that I had to get away.

Mr Tribble understood. 'Why don't you tell everybody that you're taking a long holiday, Forrest?' he said. 'The business will be here when you want it again.'

So I did. Sue came with me, and we went to the bus station.

'Where do you want to go?' the woman in the ticket office asked.

'I don't know,' I said.

'Why don't you go to Savannah?' she said. 'It's a nice town.'

'OK,' I said.

Chapter 12   Little Forrest

Sue and I got off the bus at Savannah, then I went and got a cup of coffee and sat outside the bus station. What could I do next? I didn't know. So after I finished my cup of coffee, I took out my harmonica and began to play. I played two songs – and a man walked past and threw some money into my empty coffee cup! I played two more songs, and soon the cup was half full of money!

By the end of the next week, we were getting ten dollars a day. Then, one afternoon when I was playing to some people in the park, I noticed that a little boy was watching me carefully. Then I looked up and saw a woman who was standing near him.

It was Jenny Curran.

Her hair was different, and she looked a bit older, and a bit

Then I looked up and saw a woman who was standing near the boy.
It was Jenny Curran.

tired, but it was her all right. And when I finished playing, she held the little boy's hand and came across.

She was smiling. 'Oh, Forrest, I knew it was you when I heard that harmonica. Nobody plays the harmonica like you do.'

'What are you doing here?' I asked her.

'We live here now,' she said. 'Donald works in a business here in Savannah. We came here about three years ago.'

When I stopped playing, the rest of the people walked away. Jenny sat next to me while the little boy started playing with Sue.

'Why are you playing your harmonica in the park?' asked Jenny. 'Mom wrote and told me about your shrimp business, and how rich you were.'

'It's a long story,' I said. 'Is that your little boy?'

'Yes,' she said.

'What do you call him?'

'His name is Forrest,' she said quietly. Then she went on, 'He's half yours. He's your son, Forrest.'

I looked at the boy, who was still playing with Sue. 'My . . . son?'

'I knew that a baby was on the way when I left Indianapolis,' said Jenny, 'but I didn't want to say anything. I don't know why. I was worried that perhaps –'

'Perhaps he would be an idiot,' I finished for her.

'Yes. But Forrest, he's not an idiot, he's really clever.'

'Are you sure that he's mine?' I asked.

'I'm sure,' said Jenny. 'He wants to be a football player.'

I looked at the boy. 'Can I see him for a minute or two?'

'Of course,' said Jenny, and she called to him. 'Forrest, I want you to meet another Forrest. He's an old friend of mine.'

The boy came and sat down. 'What a funny animal you've got,' he said.

'He's an ape,' I said. 'His name is Sue.'

'Why is it called Sue if it's a he?'

40

I knew then that I didn't have an idiot for a son. 'Your Mom tells me that you want to be a football player.'

'Yes,' he said. 'Do you know anything about football?'

'A bit,' I said. 'But ask your daddy. He'll know more than me.'

He put his arms round me for a second, then went off to play with Sue again.

Jenny looked at me. 'How long have we been friends, Forrest? Thirty years? Sometimes it doesn't seem true.' She moved nearer, and gave me a kiss. 'Idiots,' said Jenny. 'Who isn't an idiot?'

Then she got up and held little Forrest's hand, and they walked away.

♦

Well, after that, I did a few things. First I phoned Mr Tribble and told him to give some of my money from the shrimp business to my Mom, and some to Bubba's daddy.

'Then send the rest to Jenny and little Forrest,' I said.

That night I sat up thinking. 'Perhaps I can put things right with Jenny,' I thought, 'now that I've found her again.' But the more I thought about it, the more I finally understood that it was better for the boy to be with Jenny and her husband, and not to have an idiot for a father.

An idiot? Yes, I'm an idiot. But most of the time I just try to do the right thing.

ACTIVITIES

Chapters 1–2

Before you read

1 Look at the Word List at the back of the book. Read these questions and choose the best word.

   a Which one isn't an animal?

   ape   shrimp   jungle

   b Which one can you eat?

   banana   bet   net

   c Which one isn't a person?

   Colonel   coach   boiler   idiot

   d Which one isn't a game or sport?

   chess   wrestling   harmonica

   e Which one can you fly in?

   helicopter   bullet   medal

   f Which one can you catch fish in?

   goal   net   boiler

2 Read the Introduction to this book and answer the questions.

   a The book tells the story of Forrest Gump's life. What other story does it tell?

   b In what two ways is Forrest Gump's life like Winston Groom's life?

While you read

3 Which of these sentences are right? Tick (✓) them.

   a A box of bananas killed Forrest Gump's father.   .....

   b Forrest didn't have any friends at his ordinary school.   .....

   c He gets a place at high school because they want him in the football team.   .....

   d The trip to the cinema with Jenny goes well.   .....

   e Curtis is kind to Forrest.   .....

   f Bubba is kind to Forrest.   .....

   g Jenny is studying music at the university.   .....

4 Who says these things about Forrest, do you think? Who are they talking to?

   a 'We need him in the high school football team.'

   b 'Mrs Gump, we have your son here at the station.'

   c 'I'm sure he didn't mean to hurt her. He's a kind boy.'

   d 'He's an idiot. He comes from a stupid town called Mobile.'

   e 'He just picked it up and started to play beautifully.'

   f 'I've asked him to go for a drink with me.'

Chapters 3–4

Before you read

5 What problems are Forrest going to face in his life, do you think?

While you read

6 Who does what? Draw lines to join the people to the things they do.

   a Weasel   pays Forrest to play the harmonica.

   b Bubba   has taught Forrest to catch the ball.

   c Forrest   makes a mistake and they lose the game.

   d Jenny   puts Forrest on the bus to Mobile.

   e Coach Bryant   cries because Forrest joins the army.

   f Forrest's Mom   cooks for all the men at Fort Benning.

After you read

7 Answer these questions.

   a Who taught Forrest to play the harmonica so well?

   b Why does Forrest leave the university after a year?

   c Why does Forrest's meal for the soldiers blow up?

   d What happens to Forrest and the other soldiers when they are taking a shower?

   e Who is against the war in Vietnam?

Chapter 5

Before you read

8 Talk to other students. Do you think Forrest will be a good soldier or a bad soldier? Why?

While you read

9 Tick (✓) the things that happen.

    a The enemy soldiers blow up Forrest's machine gun.   .....

    b The enemy soldiers get between Forrest's group and the rest of the American soldiers.   .....

    c When the enemy kill Bones, Forrest takes the machine gun.   .....

    d Doyle is nearly dead and Forrest has to leave him.   .....

    e Forrest frightens the enemy soldiers when he screams and runs towards them.   .....

    f Jenny receives a letter from Forrest.   .....

    g Bubba and Forrest make plans for a shrimp farm.   .....

    h Soldiers shoot Forrest when they are crossing a field.   .....

    i Forrest runs into the rice field twice to help other men.   .....

    j Forrest doesn't remember when he got a bullet his leg.   .....

After you read

10 Work with another student. Have this conversation.

Colonel Gooch asks a soldier about Forrest Gump. The soldier tells him about Gump and Doyle and Gump and Bubba.

Student A: You are Colonel Gooch. Listen and ask questions.

Student B: You are a soldier. You were with Gump both times.

Chapters 6–7

Before you read

11 Forrest meets the President of the United States in Chapter 6. Which of these things will happen, do you think?

    a Forrest will do something stupid and everyone will be angry with him.

    b The President will give Forrest a medal and everyone will be proud of him.

12 Put these words in the correct sentences.

are killing   don't think   for helping   out with

to catch   invites   pulls down   sings with

a Mr Chi teaches Forrest Gump how .... shrimps.

b The US Army gives Forrest a medal .... other soldiers.

c A lot of young Americans .... the war in Vietnam is a good thing.

d The girl in the restaurant thinks American soldiers .... babies in Vietnam.

e The President .... Forrest to have breakfast with him.

f Forrest .... his trousers in front of the President.

g Jenny .... a group called The Broken Eggs.

h Since she left university, Jenny has been .... three different men.

After you read

13 Why does Forrest go to each of these places?

a Danang   **b** San Francisco   **c** Washington   **d** Boston

Chapters 8–9

Before you read

14 Chapter 8 is called 'Into Space'. Answer these questions.

a What kind of people usually go into space?

b If someone asks you to go into space one day, will you go?

While you read

15 Choose the right words in *italics*.

a Forrest *asks / doesn't ask* the girl to kiss him.

b Forest *is / isn't* like all Jenny's other boyfriends but she thinks he *is / isn't*.

c Jenny goes to prison because she *wants to stop the war / stole someone's medals*.

d Forrest goes to prison because he *hits one of the President's men / throws his medal away.*

e They send Forrest into space because he *is an idiot / can fly a space ship.*

f Forrest spends four years in *space / the jungle* with Sue the ape.

g Jenny is *playing with the The Broken Eggs in Boston / working at the Temperer factory in Indianapolis.*

h Forrest earns money by *arm-wrestling in a bar / betting money on fights.*

i Jenny is angry because Forrest loses a fight *purposely / by accident.*

After you read

16 Discuss these questions.

    a Does Jenny still love Forrest, do you think?

    b Why doesn't she want to live with him?

Chapters 10–11

Before you read

17 Look at the pictures on pages 33 and 36. What do you think will happen in Forrest's life as a chess player? Write your ideas.

While you read

18 Are these sentences right (✓) or wrong (✗)?

    a Forrest loses the game against the old man.   .....

    b Raquel Welch enjoys acting with Forrest.   .....

    c The best chess player in the world is a Russian called Ivan.   .....

    d Forrest takes the ape to see his mother.   .....

    e Forrest's shrimp business isn't very successful.   .....

    f Jenny is married and lives in North Carolina.   .....

    g Forrest works hard to forget his pain.   .....

After you read

19 Why are these things important in the story?

    a Forrest misses the last bus in Nashville.

    b Mr Tribble takes Forrest to see some film making.

    c Sue jumps on the chess table.

    d Forrest goes to see Bubba's parents.

Chapter 12

Before you read

20 Discuss these questions.

    a What will happen in Savannah?

    b Will Forrest end up with Jenny?

While you read

21 Who says these things, do you think? Who to? Write the names.

    a 'Have a banana.'

       .... to ....

    b 'See that man playing the harmonica? I know him.'

       .... to ....

    c 'I don't know why I came to Savannah. I can't believe you're here.'

       .... to ....

    d 'Can I have an ape for a pet?'

       .... to ....

    e 'Don't you want any of the money?'

       .... to ....

After you read

22 Choose the correct words to complete the sentences.

    a Forrest plays the harmonica in Savannah and meets Jenny and ...

       her husband   Sue   her son

    b Jenny's son is ... son too.

       Forrest's   Donald's   Rudolph's

    c Little Forrest ...

       is an idiot   doesn't like Sue   likes Forrest

d That night Forrest thinks about being with ...

Sue   Jenny and little Forrest   Mr Tribble

e He decides he shouldn't be a ... to little Forrest.

friend   idiot   father

23 Forrest says that most of the time he just tries 'to do the right thing'. Discuss these questions.

  a At the end, he says, '*it was better for the boy to be with Jenny and her husband, and not to have an idiot for a father.*' Do you think this is 'the right thing'?

  b Can you think of some other times when he does
  - the right thing?
  - the wrong thing?

24 Which of these things has Forrest done in his life? Which have you done?

  a played in a college football team

  b sung in a group

  c won a medal in the army

  d worked in a factory

  e been into space

  f won money for wrestling

  g got married

  h learned to play chess

  i written the story of his life

  j acted in a film with Raquel Welch

  k had a son

Writing

25 You are Forrest Gump's mother. Write an honest description of your son.

26 Jenny meets an old friend from school. Jenny tells her friend about her and Forrest over the years – the good things and the bad things. The friend asks lots of questions. Write their conversation.

27 Which part of the story do you think is the saddest part? Describe what happens and why it is sad.

28 Forrest plays in the Big Game at the Orange Bowl in Miami. Write about a sports game you saw or played in. What happened? Make your report exciting.

29 Look at Chapters 4 and 5 again. Find out some information about the Vietnam War and write about it.

30 Forrest meets the President of the United States on page 20. After the meeting, the President tells an assistant about it. The assistant asks some questions. Write their conversation.

31 In Chapter 9, Forrest goes into space and then gets lost in the jungle for four years. When NASA find him, a radio reporter talks to him. Write the reporter's questions and Forrest's answers.

32 Read Jenny's letter to Forrest on pages 31 and 32 again. Write Forrest's reply.

33 Do you think a story like this is a good way to learn about America and American history? Write your opinion.

34 What will happen to Forrest Gump after Chapter 12? Will Little Forrest find out about his real father? Write Chapter 13.

WORD LIST

ape (n) a large animal that can stand on two legs

army (n) a country's soldiers who fight on land

banana (n) a yellow fruit about 15 centimetres long

bet (n/v) trying to win money by guessing the result of a game

blow up (v) to destroy loudly and very suddenly

boiler (n) a large metal thing for boiling water

bullet (n) a small piece of metal that is shot from a gun

chess (n) a game; two players move their king, queen and other pieces from one square to another

coach (n) someone who trains a person or team in a sport

Colonel (n) an army officer in a high position

goal (n) in football, the place where players try to put the ball

harmonica (n) a small thing which you put to your mouth and move from side to side to make music

helicopter (n) a machine which can fly or stay in one place in the air

idiot (n) a stupid person

jungle (n) a large forest in a hot part of the world

medal (n) a small round flat piece of metal that is given to brave soldiers

net (n) a thing with lots of square holes for catching fish

shrimp (n) a small pink sea animal with ten legs that you can eat

tournament (n) a group of games; winners play against winners until there is only one final winner

wrestling (n) a sport: one person tries to push the other person down